Tell the Octopus

and other

Short Stories

Tell the Octopus

and other

Short Stories

by

Jonathan Day

DODO BOOKS

Stories

Tell the Octopus

The tentacles of the brightly coloured octopus listening to an MP3 player wound around the walls of the underpass as it snatched at musical notes floating up to the ring road above.

Crumble, who came up with most ideas, had suggested it, Anastasia, the creative one, had designed the octopus, and Tug was expert at wielding spray cans and brushes with both hands. The friends' mission in life was to paint vivid murals in impermeable colours the despair of work experience teams sent out to clean up the neighbourhood. But the town didn't need cleaning up - it needed brightening up. Crumble, Tug and Anastasia knew that their artwork would never match the wit of Banksy's but, being so good, it was seldom removed.

Anastasia's empathic spirit had been inherited from her intuitive Russian mother. Crumble (so named because of his passion for rhubarb crumble) regarded reality as a mere intrusion into his thought world: barely 22, he had the world-weary manner of someone much older. Tug (short for the tugboat which he had worked on for a couple of years) was tall, totally original and a gentleman, careful not to give offence, even when it was warranted.

They all had mundane jobs. Crumble was the proof-reader for an educational publisher, Tug a scaffolder, and Anastasia designed acrylic nails for the fingers of women who never needed to scrub a floor.

As they added the finishing touches to their octopus on the wall of the remote underpass shunned by pedestrians, they noticed Detective Inspector Knight looking down at them with that stern, unreadable expression he always wore. The three of them froze as though it would make them invisible. There was no point. This man missed nothing.

"Oh shit," murmured Anastasia.

Crumble and Tug remained like rabbits caught in the headlights even though Tug's huge tam holding his dreadlocks stood out like a Belisha beacon.

Anastasia realised that it was useless trying to pretend they were a figment of the policeman's imagination and waved cheekily. "Hi Inspector!"

"For pity's sake, Annie!" hissed Tug. "You trying to get us arrested?"

Then it occurred to Crumble that the DI had better things to do than bother with small fry like them. "He's off on important business. Look, he's wearing a hat and gloves."

And sure enough, after raising a disapproving eyebrow, DI Knight turned and strode across the ring road.

"Though that is weird."

Tug and Anastasia agreed that the taciturn upholder of the law was strange so didn't pay any attention to Crumble's comment. The DI was barely forty, yet had the presence of a 10,000-year-old glacier and depths that would have intimidated anglerfish. The friends had frequently been ordered to the police station for defacing property after being reported by some busybody or other. They were always careful to paint designs on walls that already offended the eye so their owners never filed a complaint, much preferring to keep the artwork. The friends' punishment - as such - was being hauled before DI Knight, who had more important things on his mind, to be admonished and dismissed like annoying insects with a perfunctory, "Get out and join an art class," which was the most any of them had ever heard him utter at once. He didn't need to say more; the icy glare was enough to intimidate a charging rhino.

Crumble had a theory about why the detective personally bothered to do even that. Most criminals were stupid and dealt with by uniformed police. It seemed to be the prerogative of plain clothes officers to dress down the more intelligent offenders, however inconsequential. Tug and Anastasia thought that Crumble was just flattering his own superior intellect. All the same, they decided to select more remote locations during daylight. This was one of the reasons Crumble was so intrigued to see DI Knight in his Sunday suit on a weekend by that remote underpass.

Another was that nobody accompanied him.

It didn't seem odd to Anastasia: the man must have been chilly company. "So?"

"He's up to something. By himself. On foot. Come on. Think about it."

So they did.

Anastasia's curiosity was triggered. "We've almost done here. Let's follow him."

"You crazy?" protested Tug. "We're already in enough trouble."

Anastasia quickly wiped the brushes and tossed them with their aerosols into the knapsack. She swung it onto her back, calling over her shoulder as she pursued the detective, "Come on, before we lose him."

The other two followed her through the maze of roundabout underpasses, emerging in time to see DI Knight disappear into the narrow lane leading up to the country park on its far side. Tug still doubted that it was a good idea to pursue a senior police officer on - quite possibly - a secret mission, but was outvoted by Crumble and Anastasia. He didn't actually dislike the man (Tug liked everyone), just found him intimidating in a way his companions couldn't comprehend. He didn't understand why Anastasia's mother, whenever she felt obliged to remonstrate with the police on the behalf of her artistic daughter and friends, was fascinated by the frosty DI Knight and grateful for any excuse to see him. The friends would have been amazed to learn that the detective welcomed the brief conversations they were able to have in Russian. Also, Crumble, Tug and Anastasia's artwork had a joyful exuberance even someone from a cold climate could warm to and, unbeknown to them, impressed both adults. It was unlike the pretentious daubs of many youths who had nothing better to do than make a mark on something - anything!

The police could have prosecuted the friends - they did other defacers of property - and perhaps the mural of nude cyclists in police helmets on the rear of the police station's ancient bike shed had been going a bit too far. Even though it was executed at the dead of night, their style was too unmistakable for their own good. Yet, surprisingly, it remained there!

As they darted up the lane after DI Knight, Crumble warned Tug to keep his head down. The young man was over six foot tall and conspicuous enough without the Jamaican colours standing out like a gigantic lollipop. Tug pulled off the tam and let his Rasta locks tumble out.

DI Knight didn't intend to cross the park. He continued on up towards the private, palatial properties overlooking the town. Then stopped.

Crumble, Tug and Anastasia ducked into the cover of some bushes before he glanced about to check that the coast was clear. They saw the detective enter the gate at the rear of one of the mansions and descend the steps to the property's boundary. His pursuers noiselessly dashed up the lane to peer down through the bushes. A large, affluent looking man in his sixties was waiting for DI Knight by a tool shed. Several hoes and spades were propped up against it after being cleaned. A garden fork's long, gleaming prongs pointed skywards and caught the sun's rays. This was obviously the gardener's pride and joy.

It didn't take Crumble, Tug and Anastasia long to recognise the heavy man as Archie Rogetinham, ex-mayor and outspoken critic of the council funding causes he believed charities should deal with. They knew him well. He was the one responsible for defeating the proposal to paint murals on the dreary walls of municipal buildings. They almost felt some empathy for the detective as there was obviously deep animosity between the two men.

Anastasia suddenly remembered something and looked at her watch. "How long are we going to do this? I promised mum I'd collect the groceries."

Tug took out the fob watch from his embroidered waistcoat. "It's only two o'clock. This was your idea. You got plenty of time."

"Quiet you two!" Crumble whispered urgently. "Something's going on!"

And sure enough the two men's conversation was becoming heated.

"You are tiresome and obsessive, Detective Inspector Knight. You do know why I wanted to see you, don't you?"

"You're afraid I've now gathered enough evidence to get a conviction."

"Don't threaten me, you contemptible little upstart!"

"And you'd be right."

"A fat lot of good that will do you."

The friends were fascinated to see the taciturn detective at work, cool and fearless in facing down this huge man who believed he owned everything and everyone.

"Why don't you just let this drop as your superiors told you?" Rogetinham warned DI Knight.

"They were wrong."

"Don't be so bloody arrogant! When were you promoted to chief constable?"

The detective's cool tone turned to ice. "Now I have a dossier that will ensure the arrests of you and your network of child molesters."

Crumble, Tug and Anastasia held their breath. They hadn't expected this.

The large man's voice lowered menacingly. "And, assuming that this fantasy of yours is true, what guarantee do you have that no harm would come to these young people as a consequence of you arresting me? - Theoretically of course." Archie Rogetinham had enough influence to make the threat, even against the police officer recording the conversation.

"These children have already been harmed."

"But we must assume that they are still alive - in this alternative reality of yours. Should you make any foolish move, how would you live with yourself if anything happened to them?"

The detective was unfazed by the threat. "In this 'fantasy' of mine, your octopus has a network of tentacles linked to child traffickers which stretches to the far side of the world."

Anastasia realised that the analogy with her octopus design in the underpass was not coincidental. "He knows we're here!"

The other two looked at her, horrified.

Archie Rogetinham growled menacingly. "I promise that if you come up against me in any way, children in this theoretical universe of yours would start to die."

DI Knight had no answer for that. For a second a murderous expression crossed his impassive features.

The large man laughed at the chink in the imperturbable man's armour. "And don't even think about taking the law into your own hands. If anything happens to me, the children you are so gallantly trying to protect will meet a very unpleasant fate. There is nothing you can do to prevent it but keep your mouth shut, like some of the parents who sold their children into prostitution."

Tug placed a reassuring arm about Anastasia as she attempted to keep her involuntary sobs silent. Even the unemotional Crumble seemed upset.

DI Knight looked the monster straight in the eye. "You are a foul creature. I intend to save these children from further abuse, one way or another."

"By signing their death warrants?"

"Pretending to be a respectable citizen does not put you above the law, however much influence you may have."

Archie Rogetinham gave an evil chuckle. "Oh, how naive you are, Detective Inspector. Of course it does. Haven't you learnt anything?"

"Excrement will always retain its stench, however deep you try to bury yourself and your crimes."

The large man went scarlet with rage and landed such a ferocious blow across the DI's face he was slammed against the shed. "You insolent upstart! Even your superiors know their place! It's about time you learnt yours!"

Archie Rogetinham would have launched a murderous attack if the police officer had not seized the garden fork and swung its prongs towards his attacker.

"Don't be so bloody ridiculous! You wouldn't dare!"

No sooner had the words left the huge man's mouth than he tripped and toppled forwards.

The ex-mayor and pillar of the community was impaled on the fork.

Crumble, Tug and Anastasia could see the tips of its long prongs exit the wide back, a brief spurt of blood patterning his light-coloured jacket.

Unable to take in what had just happened, the detective momentarily froze. He clutched the fork's handle in disbelief and gazed back into the horrified expression so close to his face before allowing the body to fall sideways. Archie Rogetinham lay on the ground, twitching for a moment. After the faint gurgle of blood welled up through his throat, he ceased to move.

DI Knight took off a glove to feel for a pulse in the man's fleshy neck. Crumble, Tug and Anastasia could tell by the way he withdrew that the ex mayor, and bane of creative endeavour, was dead.

"Run!" hissed Tug.

"No!" warned Crumble. "He'll see us. Even if he does know we've witnessed everything he won't want us involved. Hide over here." He pulled Tug and Anastasia into the cover of the bushes on the far side of the lane.

Seconds later the detective darted up the steps, wiped the blood away from his split lip and checked that no one was about before dashing back down the lane.

The friends came out of hiding.

Tug was worried. "Think anyone else saw?"

Crumble had already taken that into account. "No chance, the trees blocked the view from the house and we would have noticed anyone else in the grounds."

Anastasia was still trying not to sob. "But what do we do now?"

"You heard Rogetinham. If DI Knight does anything to harm him or this network of paedophiles, children will die."

"But it was an accident..."

"Like that would matter. It would be best if the death's taken as a murder committed by somebody else. If anyone finds out DI Knight was here... well... you know what will happen."

"But all those poor kids. What can we do?"

"Nothing. Absolutely nothing."

So Crumble, Tug and Anastasia reluctantly returned to the octopus in the underpass to half-heartedly add some finishing touches before going home.

Archie Rogetinham had been an important

person and his death was reported in the national news. And, just as the friends were hoping it would be declared an accident or murder by an intruder, Detective Inspector Anatoly Ilyich Knight was held on suspicion of murder. The police would not release any other details as their 'enquiries were ongoing'.

Archie Rogetinham's wife had known the exact time of her husband's secret rendezvous with DI Knight. He had demanded the detective meet him to discuss his ludicrous obsession with him being involved in a paedophile syndicate. She was well aware of the animosity between the two men and, when her husband hadn't returned to the house, immediately went down to find his body.

To make matters worse the investigating officer, Detective Chief Inspector Davis, had not been able to account for the DI's bruised face or whereabouts at that time. His mobile had been switched off and car left unattended for over two hours only a mile away.

When Crumble, Tug and Anastasia secretly met in an underpass immediately after hearing the news it wasn't to paint the walls. Two of them were near panic.

"That gang will start killing those kids!" blurted out Anastasia.

"And you heard DI Knight - they're all over the world!" added Tug.

"DI Knight said he had evidence." Crumble told them before they became irrational. "He would have put it in a safe place immediately after this happened so, if they believe that, it might buy some time. The main concern is him being charged with the murder of Archie Rogetinham.

Now Tug was near to tears. "But we have to do something!"

"So we shall," Crumble announced calmly. "If it was proved that DI Knight couldn't have committed the murder, these child traffickers would have no reason to start killing children."

"But he's hardly likely to admit it."

"In the face of the circumstantial evidence, who is going to believe him?"

"Can't we tell the police that it was an accident?" suggested Anastasia.

Crumble gave her a circumspect look. "The fact that the two men met would only confirm that he has compiled enough evidence to bring the network down. Don't forget that Rogetinham had contacts in the police who were able to suppress his previous enquiries. With DI Knight locked up, they might get to the dossier first. There is only one thing we can do - and the sooner the better."

"What's that?" asked Tug.

"Annie is sure that DI Knight knew we were watching."

"Why would that stop him thinking up something to save himself - and those kids?"

At last the truth dawned on Anastasia. "Because he's waiting for us."

An hour later the three artists approached the reception desk of the local police station.

"We have come to make a statement concerning the murder DI Knight is accused of."

The desk sergeant gave Crumble a penetrating look which warned him that this was no joking matter.

He went on in his most confident tone. "It is possible he was with us at the time."

"You mean that you are his alibi?" She sounded incredulous. "What time this was?"

"It was definitely two o'clock. We were doing this octopus in the ring road underpass when it happened…" Anastasia started to explain.

Crumble's raised hand was unable to stop her gushing on.

"And we know it was that time because I had to get back home to collect the-"

"There's no need, Annie. I'm sure we'll all be given the chance to make a full statement."

Instead of dismissing the young people for time wasting, which had been Crumble's main concern, the desk sergeant looked relieved.

She picked up her phone. "I need to speak to DCI Davies. This is important."

Crumble, Tug and Anastasia made their statements, having carefully agreed on every detail of their encounter with DI Knight beforehand. They declared that he had been struck by a half empty beer can hurled from a lorry on the ring road. (Crumble suggested the split lip and bruise had to be caused by something that unlikely because it was even less credible that this man would have tripped over anything.)

After the friends had signed their statements and told to make themselves available should any further details be required, they went away to hold their breath.

They needn't have worried. DI Knight did not contradict their story.

Shortly afterwards a news bulletin announced that the investigation implicating him had been dropped.

Weeks passed with Crumble, Tug and Anastasia living in fear of a knock at the door from some reporter or other busybody claiming to have proof of their fabricated alibi. Lie or not, it had saved the lives of some already traumatised children.

Two months later the news headlines were about an international paedophile and child trafficking ring being broken up in a joint operation by police forces across the world.

At last Crumble, Tug and Anastasia were feeling relaxed enough to plan their next artistic foray against ugly, unsuspecting walls when they received an invitation to paint a mural on the central library. A sizeable consignment of KNOxOUT paints had been donated to them by a well wisher and was awaiting collection at the council's supply depot.

The artists were shown into the room where the tins of pollution combating paints were stored. Nobody knew who had donated them, only that the order had been placed several weeks previously and the shipping manifest had no purchaser's name. There was just an envelope addressed to Crumble, Tug and Anastasia.

Anastasia opened it with an acrylic nail and pulled out a card. On it was a manga style octopus listening to music on headphones.

As she looked at it she was overwhelmed with dread.

Crumble and Tug wondered why she had suddenly become ashen.

"What's up Annie?" asked Tug. "Looks as though we did good after all. DI Knight wouldn't have spent out on all this gear if we hadn't."

"It's not that," she whispered.

"What then?" asked Crumble.

"Something's wrong."

"How do you mean?"

Anastasia couldn't say, but that cold clenching in the pit of her stomach insisted something terrible had happened. So the others accompanied her to the police station, the only place they could think of to find out what it was.

The mood inside was sombre.

Anastasia went up to the desk sergeant and asked, "What happened?"

She looked at the three friends and decided that they were entitled to know.

"DI Knight was attending a suspect's address. He was stabbed trying to release some children being held there. He died in the arms of a young girl. She thought his last words were, 'Tell the octopus that...' but English wasn't her first language and he didn't finish the sentence."

Crumble, Tug and Anastasia silently left to work on their next design.

The gable end of the library facing the High Street had scaffolding against it for several weeks as work was carried out on an elaborate mural. When the protective canvas came down, an octopus holding flowers looked down benignly on the pedestrian precinct. Its tentacles framed the portrait of someone the local residents now understood to be very special.

Their local hero, Detective Inspector Anatoly Ilyich Knight had been immortalised in pollution absorbing, permanent paint.

Apple Pie

Theo knew how to cook. Not just swirl
ingredients about in a mixing bowl and set an
oven timer. He could produce mouth-watering
meals that even his younger sister was unable to
resist, and she was the region's pickiest two-
year-old. His Greek Cypriot grandfather had
shown him the basics in his fast food café, a
business his father had refused to join, much
preferring the less greasy environment of an
office. So Theo's grandfather carried on in
anticipation of the youth losing his aspirations to
become a cordon bleu chef and rejoining the real
world in time to take his place. With each more
ambitious recipe his grandson thought up this
seemed increasingly unlikely.

Theo had set his sights on an upmarket
restaurant that catered for an elite clientele his
grandfather would never encounter over his
well-scrubbed, laminated counter. He never
mentioned this to the old man, of course, in case
he had a heart attack. But grandfather was a
pragmatist, still able to view the world in the
clear Mediterranean light he had been raised
under. Life had the knack of levelling things out
in the least expected ways, so he was happy to
let Theo contemplate the colour scheme and
seating in his small, exclusive restaurant, which
would have intimate seating and a patio
overlooking a small lake. If his grandson ever
realised his aspirations, he would be the first to
book a candlelit table and order something he

could not pronounce.

At that moment, apple pie was Theo's piéce de rèsistance. He could turn this ordinary desert into something so delectable his grandfather had tried to persuade him to make batches of it to sell in his café. Theo would have none of it. His time was firmly focused on the cordon bleu recipe book he was determined to write before his 16th birthday. Time was getting short if he was to satisfy that ambition, and the final of the Regional Young Cook of the Year Competition was coming up. His delectable apple pie was bound to win it for him. Perhaps then he might let grandfather sell it in his café to bring in the more discerning clientele, unlike the current ones who sat over a mug of tea for two hours and set the world to rights in voices that could be heard two streets away.

As well as being a talented cook, Theo was an appalling snob. No one in the family knew where this had come from: they were all down-to-earth and easy-going. Attributed to adolescent hormones, it was assumed he would grow out of it before the big, wide world knocked it out of his teenage skull.

Joining the line of hopeful competition finalists, Theo mentally dismissed the others as inadequate to the task in hand. One was dumpy with a pasty complexion, probably the result of eating too many of her own deep-fried concoctions. Another was thin and looked malnourished; the type that fretted so much about the creation of his meals he hardly dare taste them for fear of being disappointed. The third was bound to prepare a curry, her brightly coloured hijab shrieking jalapeno and hot spices.

Theo's hors d'oeuvre went well: poached salmon on a bed of finely grated fennel. The main meal was an unpretentious wild mushroom pilaf with wholemeal bread.

Then it was time for Theo's classic apple pie.

The ingredients were carefully weighed and mixed, flaky pastry gently rolled to line the ceramic dish, and apples lightly poached with cloves and nutmeg. The mixture was allowed to cool before being drained and placed on the partly cooked pastry bed. It was then covered with a sprinkling of demerara sugar and the crust laid over it before being baked. After coming out of the oven, the crust received another sprinkling of demerara. It was then ready for the finishing touch.

Theo lit his blowtorch.

Given his proximity to a very flammable roller blind, the judges looked worried and jalapeno girl tucked her hijab into her kameez.

Everyone stopped to watch this culinary artist at work, more in apprehension than admiration.

It was accepted that dangerous implements were necessary in every kitchen, even in adolescent hands, though no one had taken into account that one pair intended to use a blowtorch.

Everyone held their breath as Theo began to

caramelise the crust of his apple pie.

A sudden gust of air from the open window fanned the flame. Happily oxygenated, it did what all fire aspires to do and flared enthusiastically, so enthusiastically it set fire to the roller blind before Theo could do anything about it.

The gasp of horror was like air being sucked out of a vacuum. Judges, audience and competitors hurtled this way and that, either trying to escape or put out the fire. Theo tried to beat out the blaze with his apron, which immediately went up in flames. The roller blind was well alight so the tall, emaciated competitor yanked it from its fixings with the hook on a window pole.

A pan of boiling vegetable oil was knocked over in the confusion and ignited by the gas ring.

In the ensuing pandemonium the competitor with the pasty complexion seized a BCF fire extinguisher and brought the fire under control while one of the judges disconnected the gas and electric.

By the time the fire brigade arrived it was all over. They seemed quite disappointed. Having attended within minutes, they expected to have more to do than ventilate the stench of burnt sugar and cooking oil from the kitchen.

Theo was mortified, despite the manager of the hall reassuring him that it was well insured and needed redecorating anyway. The aspiring chef was still in shock when he was taken home by a police officer who hoped he would recover sufficiently to make a statement before the end of his shift.

Theo took to his bedroom... and stayed there.

Threats, pleading and promises could not budge him. Apart from brief forays to the bathroom and kitchen when no one was about, he remained gazing at four walls. All he appeared to eat were crisps and the cheap ginger nuts that he previously had so much contempt for. This worried his parents more than the strains of melancholy music coming from the bedroom. So they persuaded Theo's grandfather to go up and hammer on his door.

"You will open up right now, young man! This is not good behaviour!"

The one voice Theo always paid attention to was enough. The bolt was drawn back and the family elder found himself confronting the pale, drawn face of devastated youth.

"What is this?" his grandfather demanded. "You look really sick, boy?"

Theo was on the verge of tears. "I've lost my sense of taste, Granddad."

His grandfather took a deep breath. There were a few things that could be worse for a chef.

"It will return, Theo. These things happen."

"I've been eating cheap biscuits and cheese and onion crisps... And they all tasted the same as my apple pie."

"Forget your apple pie. Most people eat with their eyes and sense of smell, not their taste. Look at McDonald's; they throw out odours and bombard customers with ridiculous pictures of their meals to fool them. If everyone knew how their burgers were really produced they would be bankrupt in a week. It is all illusion. Taste is nothing." He struck his chest. "This is where it matters. You cook with your heart and people will eat."

Theo knew what his grandfather was saying. Understand the customer before thinking about the ingredients. One person's nectar could be pretentious and tasteless to most others. He had spent his young life looking in the wrong direction.

So there was no culinary degree for Theo. He went to work for his grandfather, getting to know customers, and cooking chips and garlic bread.

Fortunately, his sense of taste never fully returned.

The Puzzle Box

There was only one way to tease out this tangled thread called life - for Deanna anyway. It was to hold her breath and wish that it would all go away. It never did of course, but she always felt better afterwards. Only then did she realise that life wasn't quite tangled enough for her. The lack of intellect in others and their limited conversation was what perplexed Deanna. It was the perpetual f.....g this and f.....g that, which replaced more suitable words and, inevitably, the need to think. Her mother used the word on her children, her friends dropped it into casual conversation... and now she had heard her sainted older brother use the expletive in a radio interview - live! The star of the local football club, role model for wayward youth, and her idol since infancy had let the F word slip in public. Deanna had felt so embarrassed she dare not look him in the eye for days. Nobody else had paid any attention. As 'bloody' was regarded as offensive in the fifties, the F word was becoming just as acceptable. Deanna wanted to push a thesaurus under the noses of everyone who used it, though that would have meant felling several forests to print them.

So what could she do? Give up and join in? Try not to flinch whenever she heard it? Or go and visit Mrs Solomon, the one person guaranteed to always know the right word, correct punctuation and form of address for every dignitary you could name? Her shop of antique knick-knacks, ancient books and Tiffany lanterns between a bookmaker and mobile phone outlet sat like cut glass crystal flanked by garish plastic mugs. The odd drunk from the bookmaker would occasionally wander in to find something to squander his winnings on and, when she opened up, Mrs Solomon frequently found on the doormat mobile phones discarded by users who had upgraded. These were donated to a charity for recycling.

Deanna was one of those few visitors who helped liven up the day for the antique dealer and a panacea to the less discerning who wandered in to search for the million pound item she might have mistaken for junk - like that would happen! Mrs Solomon was able to afford her prime position in the high street and open at erratic times because of an unwavering acumen in identifying the rare and precious (her website was testimony to that). And in Deanna she could also see that rarity, a young woman who was genuinely interested in what was going on around her.

So Mrs Solomon decided to show her friend a mysterious puzzle box acquired from an inventory of goods surrendered for tax purposes. Apart from it being crafted in English yew there was little else the knowledgeable Mrs Solomon could deduce about it, even from the faded parchment concealed in a secret compartment. On it was the Georgian equivalent of a crossword puzzle with archaic clues for no doubt equally archaic solutions. The heads of the wooden keys locking the box together had strange symbols carved on them, inviting the curious to push them in the correct sequence to unlock it.

The puzzle box had been waiting under the glass counter in anticipation of Deanna's occasional, hesitant appearance. The self-effacing teenager had never quite understood why a much older person regarded her as an equal, and always felt that she was invading Mrs Solomon's authoritative space. That was the feeling most other adults gave her: they either expected appreciation for their condescending attempts to communicate with the young or deference to everything they did, however stupid. The antique dealer was a one-off, with an integrity that must have come from an interesting past history. That was why Deanna found her company so stimulating, and she really wanted to know about that past history.

The door bell tinkled its bright tune as Deanna entered the shop. The puzzle box was on the counter waiting for her, but no Mrs Solomon who must have been in her back parlour. The temptation was too great. Deanna picked up the box and prodded the ornate characters. It didn't take long for her to work out that it was a locking device.

There was a familiar voice behind her. "You know what those are, don't you?"

Mrs Solomon always moved noiselessly so Deanna should have been used to her by now, but those deep, plummy tones never failed to make her jump.

"Look like cryptic letters to me. They're either back to front or upside down so could be compositor's leads, but wouldn't print anything sensible even if they were pulled out."

"There are only 26, so are probably English."

Deanna started to jot down the layout of the letters in the notebook she always carried with her. "Yes, definitely the alphabet."

"Go for it kid. Your brain is more agile than mine." Mrs Solomon handed Deanna the ancient parchment with its list of clues to open the puzzle box. "You should be able to work out this as well."

Deanna's jaw dropped. She was good with words, but these clues in copperplate handwriting were baffling. Googling them wouldn't have helped. This called for a very old dictionary.

Mrs Solomon read her thoughts. "Samuel Johnson."

"You've got his dictionary?" Deanna asked hopefully.

"Sold the last original edition, but there is an abridged version you can use."

Deanna shook the box to check if there was anything inside. It sounded like a large key.

"Take it home with you," the antique dealer suggested.

"I'd rather not. My family is mental. It would be impossible to concentrate."

"You'd better use the back parlour then. Don't mind the cat. She'll sit on your lap, but won't be any bother as long as you let her. Keeps the knees warm."

Deanna took the puzzle box, list of clues and abridged Samuel Johnson dictionary into Mrs Solomon's parlour. As soon as everything was placed on the velvet tablecloth and she had sat down, Tabitha jumped onto her lap and made it clear with needle claws that she intended to stay there.

Deanna carefully unfolded the parchment and read the first clue:- A foul odour from Virginia: stink.

Putrid smell? Stench? She fancied there was an element of JK Rowling about it. One of her characters was quite smelly. And his name was Mundungus.

Second clue:- One part of a cloven hoof multiplied by two.

Pig, antelope, camel, satyr? No, it was more obvious than that. Separating one hoof would be to cleave. There was no cleave in this abridged dictionary, but there was clees.

Third clue:- A fowl that feeds in silt.

Could be any of a dozen birds, but Deanna doubted that Johnson was much of a twitcher, so the primary word had to be silt. A synonym for what birds waded in; marsh, water margin - Not here. A more basic term was mud. And there it was - mudsucker.

Fourth clue:- A bundle to take far.

Bundle could be a package... or, portmanteau... No. So it had to be take or far. Take was no help, so it had to be far, as in fardel.

Clue five:- A ragged fellow.

This looked easier. It was either fellow or ragged. Too many synonyms for fellow - ragged was easier, and tattered the best match. And there it was - tatterdemalion.

Now Deanna had them all. The only way to find out if her solutions were right was to spell out the words by pushing the keys on the puzzle box.

Should she do it? This device was far more fiendish than a Rubik's cube. The Georgian who designed the puzzle box must have had a lot of time on their hands. Just as it was crossing her mind that it might have been a bobby trap, Mrs Solomon pulled the parlour door curtain aside.

"You've solved it then?"

"Might have." Deanna was sure the antique dealer could have done it just as easily if she had set her mind to it but, like most adults, probably had far too many other things to do. "Would you like to open it?"

Mrs Solomon sounded genuinely impressed. "Goodness no, you solved it."

Deanna pushed in the letters to spell out mundungus. There was a 'click' as a lock deep inside the device sprang open. She hesitated, surprised that it had worked. Something this sophisticated could only have been invented by Charles Babbage and programmed by Ada Lovelace.

"Carry on," urged Mrs Solomon.

Deanna entered the other solutions. Each time another lock inside the puzzle box opened. At last tattermalion. She pushed the last letter home and sat back for fear of something leaping out at her.

With a loud 'click!' the lid sprang open and woke Tabitha. The cat's claws sank into her leg.

Nestling amongst the bars of the wooden posts was, as she had expected, a large, ornate key. Underneath it was a slip of card, battered from the vigorous shaking the box had received over the centuries. Mrs Solomon lifted Tabitha from Deanna's lap as she tipped them out.

The writing was still legible. It was an address.

"Probably demolished by now." Deanna took out her smartphone from a zipped inside pocket where she hid it from her siblings. She tapped in the address. "Couldn't be some sort of elaborate scam, could it?"

"I wouldn't know. You're probably a better judge of that given your talent to ferret things out. The nearest I get to technology is emailing the geek who manages my website."

Deanna hoped that Mrs Solomon hadn't mentioned her aptitude with electronic technology, especially in coding HTML and Java, and cracking ciphers, to anyone else. It was bound to interest dubious individuals wanting her to hack into something. The only other person to know just how good she had become was her technology teacher. Aware of how well they would get on together, he had been the one to introduce her to Mrs Solomon.

After typing the address in Start Page to reduce the number of pointless results thrown up by Google, only one mention came up. That was in a register of buildings demolished in the late 19th century.

"There's something kooky about this page." Deanna was tempted to run it though Scamadviser to see where it originated.

"How do you mean?"

Deanna checked out its source code. "It's just a page, recently posted, with too many keywords and no primary root folder. Why go to the bother of a domain name when this is all you need to upload?"

"Sorry, it's too small to see without my other glasses, and probably won't make much sense to me anyway," Mrs Solomon evaded.

"Anyway, it's quite near here. Shall we take a look?"

"Why not. I could lock the shop up tomorrow afternoon and get out the car."

"I didn't know you had a car?"

"Stays in the garage. Don't worry, I'm still safe behind the wheel. It needs an outing every now and then to keep it roadworthy." Mrs Solomon studied the location Deanna had brought up on Google maps. "Anyway, we'll never reach that by bus."

Deanna expected Mrs Solomon's car to be some old banger that she kept for its vintage value. She couldn't have been more wrong. It was hardly surprising it wasn't left parked in the road. Far from being ancient and barely roadworthy, it was the most up-to-date, top of the range, electric sports car on the market. And she thought that this woman couldn't drive!

And how the antique dealer could drive. Even the satnav had been switched off because it couldn't keep up with her.

Deanna checked their destination on Google Earth. "You do know that there aren't any buildings at this address, don't you? The nearest place is a deserted aerodrome."

"Well, we'll just take a look. The old girl likes a good spin out."

Indeed, when you had a car like Mrs Solomon's, why not let the hedgehogs know about it. The electric engine purred like a tiger as it sped across a field, startling rabbits and pheasants, to reach a potholed road leading to a long demolished house. The grounds were vast and overgrown and the occasional tower of masonry jutted above the trees.

Mrs Solomon stopped by the only intact wall. In it were steps leading down to a door.

Deanna's puzzle solving efforts hadn't been a waste of time after all.

She waited for Mrs Solomon to get out of the car before following her down the steps, tightly clutching the old key. She was sure the lock must have rusted tight after all these years.

"Did you bring a torch?" Deanna asked.

"In the car. We'll just take a peek inside first to see what's there."

"Okay." Deanna pushed the key into the lock and turned it. The tumblers immediately rotated.

Deanna started to feel apprehensive. "That's

weird." What had she let herself in for? Mrs Solomon was no longer the same amiable antique dealer she had known for over a year. As well as the expensive car and irrational diffidence about plummeting through the decaying floorboards of old ruins, her tone was now more authoritative.

"Push the door open then."

Deanna dared not refuse.

As it creaked wide, she expected a colony of bats to fly out from their roost in the decaying beams that supported the ceiling of the cellar.

Instead, a bright light flooded out onto the stone steps.

"Go in. Be careful. There's quite a drop down."

Deanna toppled into a large room. She picked herself up. Bemused operatives at computer monitors gazed at her in interest.

Mrs Solomon closed the door. "Here she is, as promised."

"She cracked it then?" a young woman exclaimed.

"Well I never! It was worth the hassle of putting that thing together after all." This voice sounded like the designer of the puzzle box. "She's better than the adults."

"Careful," chided Mrs Solomon. "She is virtually an adult."

Someone else sounded more dubious. "Still hormonal, I bet."

"No more than you when you were recruited."

Deanna was too overwhelmed to ask what

was going on.

"This is what the plebeian masses refer to as the Secret Service - technical branch," declared Mrs Solomon.

"One of those many branches they fortunately know nothing about," added the young woman.

"Meet Sangeeta," announced Mrs Solomon. "She will induct you into the ways of our little world - should you be interested."

Overcoming her amazement, Deanna could only think of one thing. "But how did you all get down here? There's no proper road or car park."

"There, what did I tell you. Picks up on things that matter."

Sangeeta laughed. "There is a tunnel to the aerodrome. Built during the last war. Once the walls were reinforced and wildlife evicted, it was ideal for our little bolthole, well away from phone masts."

"Then how do you receive and transmit?"

"All cabled up to our own exchange. No Wi-Fi down here."

"But if all this is a supposed to be secret, why are you letting me see it?"

"Don't worry," the dissenting voice chimed in. "We'll just shoot you if you tell anyone else."

"Shut up Dancy!" scolded Mrs Solomon. "The only person I'm liable to have shot is you."

Deanna wandered uncertainly about the room lined with monitor screens, trying to guess what the software was capable of.

"Well," snapped Dancy, disregarding Mrs

Solomon's glare, "want to join us or not?"

"Will I need to shoot anyone?"

"Only Dancy," said Mrs Solomon.

"But I'm not 16 yet?"

"You can still the sign the secrets act."

"What will my parents say? They'd never allow it."

"We're a secret service - you don't tell them. You'll be 16 in four weeks and able to do what you like - mostly."

"Can I tell my brother?"

"You mean the one that let the F word slip on live TV?"

"You saw that then, did you?"

"Brilliant football player, but not so bright. We're only interested in wordsmiths and have a very large swear box. Leave him to his boozy friends and blissful oblivion of what happens in the big, wide world." Mrs Solomon indicated the monitors. "And this, believe me, is the big, wide world the tabloids do not have the words to describe. What we do might scare them to death. Not you, though. I reckon you'll be here for keeps."

Roy Goes On a Trip

It was the largest mushroom Roy had ever seen. It shouldn't have been there, rooted between the cracks of the crazy paving. Even more worrying was its smug expression; an impudent, marshmallow face grinning up at him.

Roy almost smiled back in surprise, but managed to control himself. When hundreds more grinning mushrooms popped up, he decided things were getting too strange and fled up the path towards a grotto.

As Roy approached, the shell encrusted entrance turned into gaping jaws - which swallowed him whole.

The belly of the grotto was alive with liquid creatures lapping about his knees, trying to digest him. The more he struggled, the lower the fossil encrusted ceiling descended. On the verge of being crushed, he was catapulted into a world of prehistoric beasts. Fleet-footed carnivores with beady yellow eyes were hunting gigantic browsers the size of cathedrals. Then the predators turned and saw the young interloper, a much easier lunch than a massive brontosaurus.

The flock of deinonychus surrounded their new meal, snapping at him hungrily. Roy closed his eyes tightly, and would have clicked his heels three times to wish himself back home if he had been wearing Dorothy's ruby slippers. But the ploy worked and once again he found himself in a different dimension. It wasn't Kansas or the

Land of Oz, though the faces now surrounding him were more familiar.

Kat had always reminded him a little of a meat eating raptor, though given the state of his teeth he probably wasn't that dangerous. The gang that tagged along behind the nasty little lout were regarded as life's losers rather than the terror of the neighbourhood, which made Kat even more obnoxious. He put his ugly face too near Roy's. Roy punched it and saved the dentist the trouble of having to extract a couple of rotten teeth. No sooner had the blow landed than the switch controlling his progress through this weird otherworld rotated a couple more notches.

He was standing on a high peak. Below, beetling-browed faces in the rock glowered up and threatened to scream in rage. For fear of falling down one of their throats, Roy jumped in the hope this bad dream would allow him to fly. Instead he landed in a gullet that immediately tried to swallow him. The nightmare now seemed too real as it began to turn into the most visceral, violent video game made flesh.

Roy tried to yell out, but that was strangled in his throat as razor sharp talons snatched him from the devouring face in the rock. He was carried into a stratosphere filled with pumpkin-shaped creatures wearing gnomish expressions like the mushrooms.

Their smiles gaped wide to reveal tunnels into black treacle oblivion.

The talons released Roy into the nearest cavernous mouth and he tumbled, panic stricken, into a glutinous, soul-devouring, black ocean. Huge shapes butted him this way and that until he was sucked down into a deep sump where dark energy gathered up quantum detritus. This was the toilet at the end of the Universe.

Something massive was bouncing on his chest.

And there were words.

"Keep going Mavis or we'll lose him."

There was an exasperated voice. "Stupid little idiots - why do they do it?"

A flashing blue light briefly penetrated Roy's eyelids before the pumpkin creatures returned to chase him, followed by the rock faces, Kat and his gang, dinosaurs and, eventually, marshmallow-faced mushrooms.

"He's back Sid. Let's get him into the wagon."

Then the throbbing started. Roy could feel his whole body rise and fall with each nauseous spasm. He was crashing through doors, being tossed from trolley to table, from table to bed, from bed down a bottomless pit filled with huge, writhing worms.

Then came real pain.

He screamed.

"We have to get that stuff out of his stomach before we can deal with the fractures," a calm voice decided.

There was the jab of a hypo in his thigh and the writhing of the worms turned into a sedate waltz as his stomach was turned inside out.

"Next of kin?" Another voice called out.

"Being informed."

"They needn't rush. He'll be in the operating theatre for some time."

A mask was placed over Roy's face and at last his nightmare came to an end.

The next voice he heard sounded distant. By its edge of authority it wasn't a nurse.

"Come on, give the doctors a clue, love. What drugs were you doing?"

"Dunno," he murmured. "Friend gave it to me."

"What? Again? Just who is this friend of yours? If we can't do him for supplying drugs, he should be prosecuted for being a twerp in charge of a chemistry set."

Roy managed to focus on the young woman taking notes. So far she had only managed to jot down 'unresponsive'.

"What happened?" he groaned.

"Long or short version?"

"Can't remember."

"Short version then?"

"Tell me?"

"You thought you were Batman and tried to fly off the balcony of your flat. Pity you didn't remember that it was three floors up."

The Handbag Gang

The tapestry flowers embellished with sequins was Lorraine's favourite, closely followed by the embossed olive velvet and linen embroidered with thistles and cornflowers.

It was an odd hobby for a 15-year-old, collecting handbags and other accessories, especially as few of them were ever used. It was just as strange that her two closest friends, Sam and Toby, shared the same passion. Every season they would display their collection at a local bazaar to buy, sell and exchange handbags, brightly coloured silk scarves, and gloves. Leather and plastic were banned. Every item had to be fabric; linen, velvet or canvas, lovingly hand embellished with appliqué, needlepoint, embroidery or beads, and very colourful.

Sam had the skill to mend, make and create new items, an ability inherited from her mother who was a florist expert at designing wreathes and bespoke greetings cards for every occasion. Toby was 16 and had a steady boyfriend, but that did not interfere with her dedication to fashion accessories. In fact, Luke was happy to help out, searching for antique handbags, scarves and gloves in charity shops and boutique sales.

And it was Luke who made that extraordinary discovery. None of the friends had seen a handbag quite like it before, its iridescent satin catching the light like butterfly wings.

It also had zipped compartments. When Luke

had searched each one in the charity shop they were empty. The mere fact that someone had donated something this expensive was remarkable in itself. Expecting them to leave valuables inside it as well was a little too much to hope for, but Lorraine needed to make sure that the odd diamond had not been caught in a seam. She rummaged about the handbag's interior and pulled out a black velvet cube.

"But I went through it thoroughly," protested Luke, "and nobody but us has touched it since. It's not one of you having a joke, is it?" He knew that the Handbag Gang was too dedicated to waste time on playing tricks like that, but it seemed to be the only explanation.

Lorraine placed it on the trestle table with their recent acquisitions. "What is it? Looks like a jewellery box, but doesn't seem to open. It's too large for a key ring and doesn't have a link to attach it to anything else."

"Perhaps it's a demon taxi driver's fluffy dice," suggested Toby.

The four of them stood gazing at the mysterious black cube.

Then it moved - very slightly, but just enough to make them jump.

"My God! It must have batteries," exclaimed Luke.

"It's an electronic toy of some sort," Toby agreed. "Perhaps it operates by Wi-Fi."

"To do what?"

The words were hardly out of Luke's mouth when its sides opened.

Like a piece of origami, huge, iridescent petals unfurled.

"Oh that is too weird!"

The four friends backed away as the cube rapidly increased in size and exuded a grey duvet of mist.

The room grew dark.

Lorraine, Toby, Sam and Luke would have dashed out if they could find the door.

Then the ghostly mist dissipated and the room returned to normal. The cube resumed its original shape, as innocent as a fur fabric dice dangling in the windscreen of a taxi, albeit driven by a demon.

The Handbag Gang refused to discuss what had happened. None of them indulged in illegal substances or was prone to hallucinations, so embarrassment inhibited them from talking about it.

Months passed. It did not occur to them that the odd experience had been responsible for the sudden burst of energy that had encouraged them to transform their innocent interest in fashion accessories into a serious business. They called their new brand Butterfly Designs.

Within a couple of years the young adults were supplying accessories on eBay to brighten up drab society. They soon had the funds to expand into clothing and their designs were mass produced for the high street outlets they established. Their commitment to colour and decoration became an obsession. They did not understand why, when people were more affluent than they had ever been before, they dressed in such dull, uniform colours. The chemicals that enabled modern textiles to be dyed in brilliant, exotic shades had never been used to their full advantage in the West. Designers, especially those of the major stores, seemed committed to the dull end of the spectrum as though anything else would scare off the customers. Even the fruit and vegetables on supermarket aisles had better colour coordination than the clothing department.

Lorraine, Toby, Sam and Luke were determined that fashion should embrace bright hues to reflect the glorious world they lived in.

After five years of trading, the entrepreneurs were controlling a huge clothing empire with outlets across Europe. At first fashion magazines had ranted at their unsubtle blending of colours. Butterfly Designs ignored the outcry. Their skirts, jackets, trousers, shirts, frocks and blouses were spangled with beads, sequins, embroidery and appliqué. And then - horror of horrors - they designed a catalogue of bright, brash clothes aimed at the senior market. People in their eighties deserted M&S and wore vivid, clashing colours to demonstrate their lack of respect for convention and drably dressed members of younger generations.

Soon, bright colours were everywhere.

Schools changed the compulsory grey, navy blue and dark green uniforms for rainbow colours which pupils could mix and match. Military designers suggested silver braid and buttons on lavender for a range of dress uniforms, but were promptly reprimanded before they started adding sequins to combat gear.

No longer just a fashion statement, brightly coloured clothes, from Bermuda shorts to burkhas, became the norm across the globe. Rich and poor alike now felt free to express their individuality in the way they dressed whether neat or sloppy. People became happier, more confident, and satisfied with life. Cases of depression dropped and mindless crime became rarer.

Lorraine, with her new partner Larry, Sam, resolutely single, Toby, now married to Luke, decided to take stock of what they had achieved in ten years. Each of them was so wealthy they could have spent the rest of their lives in indolent luxury if they had chosen to. None of them would have admitted it, but they had joined the self-satisfied elite that at one time they had taken such delight in ridiculing with their outrageous designs. The Handbag Gang no longer wore the clothes they had created. Everything was haut couture, tasteful and very, very expensive. Perhaps it was time to retire and let the huge clothing empire they had established float on the stock exchange.

Those early, precious items they had collected before launching Butterfly Designs had been lovingly packed away. Now it was time to remove everything from the crates stored at Lorraine's mansion and decide whether it should be retained to litter the interiors of their immaculate, palatial homes.

The beaded and embroidered handbags were first to be pulled out. Then Luke came across the iridescent, satin bag that he had discovered so long ago.

There was something inside it, so he shook it out.

A black velvet cube fell onto the polished pine floor and bounced against the crystal encrusted geode Lorraine had collected in South America.

"What's that?" Toby asked.

Luke shrugged. "Don't know. Can't be worth anything."

"Chuck it away then."

"Okay." Luke opened the door of the stove in the centre of the open plan room and tossed the cube into it.

The change was imperceptible at first. Then slowly colour began to leach away from everything; their fine clothes, furnishings, and even the garden furniture outside.

For a moment the companions hardly noticed.

Their world was losing its rainbow hues to reflect the dull state of mind they had dwindled into.

As colour seeped away from the world, with it went the friendly smiles of strangers. The world's pessimistic outlook returned, so did the petty squabbles, intolerance and murderous wars.

That night the small cube sat in the dying embers of the fire. It shook the ash from its velvet skin like a small dog, and then shot up the flue and out into the dark sky embroidered with nebulae, gas giants and diamond stars.

Threep!

It was not much taller than Jenny and sprouted hair like a startled floor mop.

Most disconcertingly, it went, "Threep!"

The sound was far from birdlike and demanded a response.

"Hello," said Jenny.

"Threep!"

The creature fiddled with an array of buttons on its baggy, blue overalls. "Hello," it eventually said.

"Who are you?" asked Jenny. She knew it was wrong to talk to strangers, but this creature was so strange it was hard to resist.

"My-code-is-Omega-20-in-your-language."

"What does that mean?"

"I-am-the-last."

"The last of what?"

"It-is-complicated."

Adults always seemed to use that excuse when they didn't want to explain something.

"My name is Jenny. I'm eight. How old are you?"

"My-allocation-has-no-time-frame."

Well, Omega 20 certainly sounded like an adult.

"What are you doing here?"

"Observing."

Jenny looked about them. There was nothing much to observe beyond the hedgerows and farm outhouses. It was always entertaining to watch Matron, the sow, wallowing, but she was now inside suckling a litter.

"Observing what?"

At last something Omega 20 didn't have an answer for.

With a whirring sound punctuated by several "Threeps!" the strange creature disappeared.

How odd, thought Jenny. Those students employed during the summer must have been playing a joke. Either that, or filming a science-fiction movie. Her family always used to play jokes until, without warning, they became very serious. A few weeks ago, Jenny had arrived home from her cousin's and thought she had been brought back to the wrong house. Nobody was the same. Paul, older brother, no longer heaped sugar into his tea; Buster, the dog, instead of rushing to greet everyone at any pretext, was slinking away as though they were liable to kick him. The worst thing was the change in her mother. She no longer smiled, just looked vacuous as though newly arrived from a different planet.

Jenny was still given breakfast, lunch and dinner, made to get up in the mornings and sent to school, but there was no more home-made ice cream, plum jam or evening trips to the supermarket. All the joy had drained from her family. It was hardly surprising the eight-year-old was starting to see strange creatures that went "Threep!"

To make matters worse, Bob and Sid had left without warning at the same time, leaving her father and brother to manage the farm by themselves.

Money had always been tight, so the family was dependent on her mother's salary for shelf stocking at the very supermarket that took forever to pay for their calabrese and trimmed parsnips. However much Jenny's parents moaned about that, they always used to laugh it off as the price for being blessed with such a wonderful view over the Downs. That was usually followed by ribald comments about Matron being less greedy than company directors who must have had similar waistlines. Now they weren't bothered one way or another.

Then the morning after meeting "Threep!", a new farmhand arrived.

Hopefully she would lighten the atmosphere once everyone didn't need to work so hard. The young woman certainly had the physique to carry sacks of parsnips and turn the screw on the apple press come cider season.

"What's your name?" Jenny demanded before she allowed her inside the farmhouse.

The new farmhand smiled. "Ollie."

"That's an odd name?"

"You are Jenny, aren't you?"

Jenny was puzzled. She had never met Ollie before and was sure her parents weren't communicative enough at that moment to have told her.

"Have you had breakfast? Everyone else has, but I can scramble some eggs before I go to school if you like?"

"There's really no need."

"All right. I don't know where the others are, so I'd better show you to Sid's old room. You wouldn't like Bob's. He was a mucky old bugger."

The young woman smiled.

That was unusual. Most adults showed disapproval when the eight-year-old swore, but Ollie seemed to assume that it was the most natural thing in the world.

"Thanks."

After the new farmhand had unpacked and freshened up, there was still no one else to meet her.

Before Jenny dashed for the school bus she thrust a sheet of paper into her hand. "This was on the kitchen table. Looks like dad left you a list of things to get on with."

"Thank you Jenny. You have been very helpful."

Ollie watched the schoolgirl dash up the lane just as her bus came over the brow of the hill.

She waited until it was out of sight, tossed away the list of things to do and opened her jacket to take out a small tracking device. The high pitched signal it emitted woke Buster. He came charging across the farmyard, wondering how he had missed the arrival of the newcomer. There was something very wrong here. He growled and kept a safe distance as she strode away from the farm.

Ollie used the detector's beam to sweep a small clearing. Human forms started to take shape - two adults and a young man. They remained nebulous, obviously not aware of anything.

She scanned the area again. This time two bodies appeared on the ground. They immediately became solid and appeared to be dead. Ollie removed another device from her jacket and used it to pulse a shaft of energy at them.

Sid coughed and came to with a jolt. "What the hell!" Then he saw Bob lying beside him, apparently lifeless. "Oh my God!"

Ollie pulsed energy at the motionless body until it moved.

Sid pulled Bob up into a sitting position. "Wake up you old fool! I thought you were dead! I nearly shit myself!" Then he became aware of Ollie standing there. "Who the hell are you?"

"What is the last thing you remember?"

Sid had to think. "Mucking out the old Matron and her litter." He looked at Bob. "Gord knows what he was doing. Probably having a quiet smoke behind the tool shed."

Hearing Sid's rasping tones, Buster bounded into the clearing and bounced on the two dazed farm hands. Then the long-haired spaniel saw the shadowy forms of the family and whimpered in terror.

"What happened to them?" demanded Sid.

"You must tell me what happened," Ollie insisted. "Otherwise I can do nothing to help them."

But something else occurred to him. "Jenny's not with them? She okay?"

"She is safe. Tell me what happened?"

"It's all a bit of a fog." Sid managed to get to his feet. "I'd just filled the old Matron's swill and was coming back to feed the hens... There was something in the yard..."

"Please concentrate."

"Only it wasn't really there."

"What colour was it?"

"What?"

"Bright yellow, dark blue, pink, hadrinaceous..?"

"Hadri... what?" Sid remembered. "A sort of red smog glowing like a furnace. There were things inside it."

Infrared; that's what Ollie needed to hear. It meant that there may still be time.

Sid indicated the three frozen figures. "They alright?"

"That depends..."

"Who the bleeding hell are you?"

Ollie didn't answer. She turned and walked back to the farm.

Bob struggled to his feet and Sid helped him follow her, neither sure whether it was such a good idea.

By the time they reached the yard the mysterious woman was sweeping the area with her small scanner. Finding nothing, she went into the farmhouse kitchen. When Sid and Bob reached her and looked inside, the stones of its ancient chimney breast were glowing red. They didn't recognise this as the place where they used to sit and eat their meals.

The Welsh dresser displaying decorative

51

plates had been replaced by a peculiar honeycomb structure filled with busy, buzzing lights. The large oak table was now a dome of octagonal cells from which tiny entities came spinning out, weaving nebulous webs.

"Bloody hell! What's going on?"

"Keep back!" Ollie warned Sid.

She was standing in the midst of the furious swarm, apparently impervious to their attacks.

Bob was still only half aware of what was going on and assumed he was hallucinating. "What's up Sid?"

Sid's common sense told him to get out of there, but curiosity had him rooted to the spot.

Just as he thought Ollie would be consumed by the dense webs and buzzing swarm, the room was filled with a flash of brilliant light.

The strange hive and furious entities disappeared.

So did the woman.

Where she had stood was an alien in blue, baggy overalls and hair like an exploding floor mop.

"Who the thundering hell are you?" Sid demanded.

"Omega-20."

The alien pushed a button on her baggy overalls, and was gone.

When Jenny came home her parents, brother, Sid and Bob were sitting around the kitchen table looking bewildered.

Buster was underneath it, whimpering with

confused delight.

The eight-year-old had come to expect no friendly greeting on arrival and tossed her satchel onto a chair. She went to the sink to pour a glass of water. Without warning her mother leapt up and gave her a hug that knocked the breath out of her.

"Still with us then, kid?" called Paul as though wondering why she hadn't run off long ago.

"It's alright Jen," reassured her father, "we're all back to normal."

"Though where the hell we've been none of us knows," added Sid.

Jenny was aware someone was missing. "Where's Ollie?"

"Ollie? Was that the woman's name? She turned into this peculiar creature and said her name was really Omega 20."

So Jenny hadn't imagined the alien after all.

"Don't worry about it Jen," Sid told her, though knew he would have nightmares for the rest of his life. "Everything's alright now."

After the Matron had been fed and bedded down for the evening and the others were watching TV, Jenny secretly slipped out and went to the spot where she had met Omega 20 or "Threep!" as she remembered it.

There was still a strange electrical charge in the air.

"Where are you?" she called.

Omega 20 shimmered into view against the setting sun.

"What happened?" There was urgency in the eight-year-old's tone that refused to be fobbed off with some adult platitude.

"Parasites. They-infest-other-lifeforms-and-use-their-energy-to-reproduce. They-create-replicas-of-their-victims-to-avoid-detection."

"Ugh! How disgusting."

"Your-family-was-cleansed-before-they-could-be-drained."

"Didn't the parasites want Sid and Bob then?"

"They-must-have-sampled-them-and-not-liked-the-taste."

Jenny could understand that. Bob smoked like a chimney and Sid lived off burgers and beer.

"Where are you going now then? Home to a different planet?"

"This-is-my-planet. I-was-installed-here-after-the-dinosaurs-died-out."

Jenny couldn't believe her ears. "You mean the dinosaurs were wiped out by these parasites?"

Omega 20 had told her enough. "I-must-go-now." And with a brief "Threep!" disappeared.

Door in the Wall

There was a door in the wall.

It had always been secured with a padlock, but this evening the shackle had not been pushed home.

Ben lifted the padlock from the hasp and opened the door. He had no idea what was on the other side, he only knew that he needed somewhere to sleep for the night. Several interlopers had moved into the underpass and they were beginning to attract too much attention. With only one or two of the regulars dossing down there, the locals didn't feel threatened and passed by without comment. Now, to make matters worse, a local gang had started to loiter at the end of the underpass, obviously with trouble in mind. None of the regulars - or interlopers - were in a fit enough state to fend off an attack and the police, when they did turn up, would only find a few bloodied victims and bedding strewn the length of the tunnel.

That scared Ben more than the unknown on the other side of the secret door. He peered in and could just make out what seemed to be a storeroom beneath the University campus car park. It was dry, secret, and would suit him for those few risky hours before dawn.

He could find no light switch, so took out the old windup torch given to him by a well-wisher and went inside. There was another door in the far wall, but Ben was too tired to explore. He tossed his bedding into a corner, replaced the open padlock in the hasp of the outer door and pulled it to. It was unlikely anyone else would notice. Not even students visited the rear of the university grounds bordering the railway sidings where there was nothing but ragwort and piles of ballast for the tracks. Ben was the only one of his group who still had enough curiosity to investigate such unlikely places. He was a survivor. In fact, given his young years, he had survived enough adversity for several lifetimes.

That had taken its toll. Ben was always exhausted. He fell asleep as soon as his head hit the rolled blanket he used as a pillow. When outside he usually managed to wake before the owner of the shop whose porch he was dossing down in arrived to open up. Most business owners took exception to down and outs using the front of their shops as dormitories, the more fastidious scrubbing the tiles with disinfectant as a precaution against fleas, scabies and Ebola.

Ben felt secure enclosed in the pitch darkness of his new hideaway. He carried on sleeping until morning when a noise on the other side of the internal door roused him. It sounded, and felt, as though something was drilling deep into the ground. Surely the University wouldn't allow an oil company to drill beneath its campus? The students would have rioted if they found out. Ben pulled the half bottle of flat Lucozade from his knapsack and took several swigs to wake himself up. He quickly rolled up his bedding and delved about in the bottom of his knapsack for the discoloured eraser, which often proved useful when finding a new bolthole from the unfriendly night. He sliced a sliver from it with his penknife and packed it into the padlock keyhole. It didn't work every time, but anyone careless enough to not secure the shackle wouldn't notice that the tumblers had not engaged.

After a quick glance about outside to make sure the coast was clear, Ben pulled the door to after him and replaced the padlock in the hasp.

First things first. He needed to find out how his acquaintances had fared the night before in the underpass.

As soon as he arrived it was obvious that it had not been well. A uniformed PC was watching several smug faced youths. He caught Ben's eye and indicated he should take a different route. After making a mental note of the thugs responsible for the mayhem of the previous night, Ben followed the PC's advice and doubled back to find some biscuits for breakfast at the food bank - Bourbons if they had them.

The next night, safely behind the door in the wall, Ben felt guilty at not sharing its location with the others attacked in the underpass the previous night. But that was a law of the street; survival first, friends in adversity, second.

Again Ben was woken by drilling. It was much louder this time. A quick glance outside told him that the sun was about to rise and in the light of his windup torch he could see steam seeping under the inner door. Unlike others who were ethanol dependent, he didn't imagine things. Ben's dreams might have been turbulent, but they weren't about subterranean hells. He had to know what was going on down there. A slight push at the inner door opened it slightly.

Light and steam flooded the storeroom, giving Ben an instant sauna. It was impossible to see what was happening below. Against his better judgement, he had to find out. There was a metal walkway, which fortunately had a railing to prevent its users plunging into the shaft where the drilling was taking place. Ben carefully eased his way along it, hoping to catch a glimpse of what was going on beneath the steam. He had been an apprentice engineer before having to hit the road and understood geothermal energy. This steam was being generated by water being pumped from deep in the ground. The University above wasn't only researching solar and wind power. Since the fracking controversy, which involved sinking boreholes under people's property, it was hardly surprising they were keeping quiet about this project. Perhaps the new uni had chosen its isolated location to test their experimental drilling rig, albeit at an ungodly hour in the morning, and not just to give refuge to down and outs. What next? Admit they had been drilling without authorisation, or create a company to declare the success of a cheap new way to sink bores at a 'future' date?

For the first time in years Ben felt engaged with something. This was far more important than the thugs terrorising his companions or wondering where the next meal would come from. He had to see more and felt his way through the steam.

Further along the walkway there was another door. He pushed it open and a brilliant shard of light from the rising sun cut through the steam. Ben quickly dodged outside before someone below noticed, jamming his foot in the door to ensure it didn't slam shut on him.

Shading his eyes from the rising sun, he found he was standing by the disused bridge over a derelict railway station.

Propping the door open with a brick, Ben went to investigate this forgotten, derelict corner of railway history where trains were being moved from their sidings to collect the first passengers of the day. Even the drivers shunting the engines from their night-time berths under the rusting footbridge probably didn't give this deserted platform and overgrown tracks beyond it a second glance. They were all that remained of a branch line after the Beeching cuts. Ben decided against crossing the bridge over the trains below. Its supports were rusty and the screws half hanging out of them.

The sun was getting higher so he returned to the storeroom. He rolled up his bedding, replaced the sabotaged padlock, and left to find breakfast.

No one slept in the underpass any more. Even the hardiest of its night-time residents had taken police advice and accepted beds at a hostel. The local thugs had lost an easy target to terrorise, but were not yet willing to risk injury by fighting another gang. Without their ringleader, Conan, they would have gone back to spraying graffiti and playing Grand Theft Auto. The bodybuilder had crossed Ben's path two years previously when he had been fit enough to fend him off. Now Ben wouldn't have stood a chance. All he could do was keep looking over his shoulder and ensure he was safely in his bolthole before the streetlights were turned off. Conan might not have possessed a great intellect, but knew how to hold a grudge.

Several nights passed, Ben snug in his secret hideaway and the others safely under a charity's roof.

As dawn broke one morning, Ben took his regular stroll along the walkway through the steam and out to view his secret kingdom on the far side of the derelict station. He felt uneasy. He didn't know why. But that instinct for survival was finely honed and never ignored. He went back to the storeroom, rolled up his bedding and quickly left.

Turning the corner from the university's entrance were a student and older man. They headed to the storeroom door. Ben wondered why they were there so early in the morning and tried not to panic. What if they found out the padlock had been sabotaged and had it replaced? No more refuge for the night.

He darted behind the bushes on the other side of the road and watched the couple enter the storeroom. At least leaving earlier than usual meant he hadn't been caught.

Then Ben's worst nightmare appeared. His early-morning foreboding had also saved him from encountering Conan. The only reason the thug had for being there was because he had discovered Ben's secret hideaway. Now the chance to sleep there again had really gone.

Ben's immediate instinct was to run and not come back. Then a sickening thought stopped him. It was dark in the storeroom. Conan wouldn't have thought twice about beating up the elderly professor and his young female student if he believed that they were getting between him his quarry. There was no way to contact the police. Everywhere was deserted and the credit on Ben's last mobile had expired months ago.

Conan entered the storeroom.

Ben pulled a metal strut from the ancient railings holding back the bushes and darted across the road.

There were raised voices, and then a girl's scream.

Ben hurtled to the storeroom and threw the door wide like an emaciated fury. There was blood on the old man's face after he had attempted to come between his student and Conan.

The bodybuilder had the girl by the arm and would have struck her as well if Ben had not lashed out with the metal bar. Conan fell back. This gave Ben just enough time to open the inner door and dash through it, shouting obscenities over his shoulder to ensure that the thug chased him.

The body builder charged like an enraged bull along the metal walkway and out of the other door.

Ben was already running across the rusty bridge, over the trains being shunted out to their stations, and down to the derelict platform. He jumped onto the disused tracks and hid amongst the buddleia colonising them. Conan assumed he had dashed off into the wilderness beyond and loped along to the far end of the platform.

Taking his chance, Ben jumped back up and onto the bridge. But Conan saw him leave his hiding place and charged after him. Ben's intention had been to get inside and slam the door shut before he could reach it. By the time Conan had discovered a way round to the door of the storeroom, he and the other two would be well away. But one of Ben's torn trainers snagged on a loose tread.

He went sprawling.

With a roar of triumph, Conan pounded his way across the bridge towards him.

It shuddered dangerously.

Suddenly Ben felt helping hands pulling him clear of the rickety structure as the bridge's struts snapped.

It turned turtle, pitching Conan onto the rails below. Dazed and disorientated, he managed to get to his feet and spin round just in time to see the carriages bearing down on him.

The look of amazement on Conan's face shortly before he was mangled by their wheels would live with Ben forever. The driver at the far end of the train may have felt a slight bump, but obviously wasn't aware that he had struck anyone. Why would he have been? There was never anybody about at that time of day. He was even less aware of Ben, the professor and his student gazing down in horror at the bloody tangle of what had once been a bodybuilder.

Their appalled silence continued until Ben's sense of self-preservation kicked in. He ushered the professor and his student back inside.

They had to decide what to do. Telling the police what had happened would have meant revealing the University's illicit research into geothermal energy. The consequences would have been the loss of numerous grants at best, and prosecution at worst.

Ben knew that nothing much would happen if he told them about Conan. The police were aware that he wanted to kill him and it would be plausible he died attempting to do it. Ben would either spend several nights in a warm cell with full board, or they would shake his hand.

Despite being convinced that the young man knew what he was doing, the other two were reluctant to leave him to shoulder the responsibility of what had happened. But Ben insisted: his life was already screwed up, there was no point in the same thing happening to the student, so the professor handed Ben his card with instructions to call him.

After the professor and his student had returned to the University, he picked the eraser from the padlock, pulled the door of the storeroom to, put the shackle through the hasp and snapped it shut. His knapsack and bedding were well hidden in the bushes opposite and he could retrieve them at any time.

Ben followed the perimeter of the University's grounds, back to the sidings and derelict station. The bridge was now hanging precariously from a couple of loose bolts over where Conan's body lay. Ben scrambled down the crumbling wall it was attached to and ran along the track to attract the attention of the driver shunting the last passenger carriages from their overnight berth. He frantically gabbled out that the bridge had collapsed and there was a body on the track. Within minutes the yard was locked down. Nothing moved until the railway police arrived.

Ben's explanation that Conan had been chasing him seemed plausible enough - it was unlikely to have been the other way round. He didn't even need to spend a night in a cell which, given that he had lost his regular spot, was inconvenient. However, after hearing what had happened, his companions in the hostel were only too willing to have him join them. With Conan gone they could safely move back to the underpass.

Ben had been through so many institutions during his early life, he had never expected much. The engineering apprenticeship was the most he had ever expected to achieve before fate intervened, and he hadn't anticipated anything more than a thank you when he did find a phone to call the professor. Those who have never had much expect little and have nothing to lose. But Ben did not count on the professor rating his IQ above average. So much so that, after explaining their geothermal drilling project to the young man, the professor managed to procure a grant for him to work with his legitimate research group. Despite Ben's early training as an engineer, his skills were far from university standard, and he expected the job to be sweeping floors or cleaning condensation from the walls of the secret research chamber. But his brain had not been addled by drugs or booze and his prospects turned to be more promising. Best of all was having a warm bed for the night.

The Changeling

There was not much that could be said to the mother whose newborn had just died in her arms. Yet the ancient, upright man visiting her had sparkling eyes that expressed more than words.

The small stranger lifted a slender hand.

Life returned to the frail infant. Her fair wisps of hair took on the colour of flame and an otherworldly beauty pervaded the baby's features.

"How did you do that?" whispered Emma. "The doctors said there was no hope."

"She will now be with you for 12 years and a day. Bring her to me before that birthday."

Emma and Todd were so elated at having a child survive after so many stillbirths they did not worry about the implications of the pact they had just made. There was something of a holy man in this mysterious hospital visitor's demeanour and honeyed tone of voice. They did not doubt him for one moment, let alone question how he had performed the miracle that flew in the face of medical diagnosis

"Do not lose this." The small man held up a golden card. "On it is the address you must bring her to. Be sure that it is on the date inscribed on the reverse."

Todd took the card and put it in his wallet, and then turned to hold the daughter he thought he would never have. "Hello Gingie."

Neither he, nor Emma, noticed the

diminutive magician leave as enigmatically as he had appeared.

There was a lawn on the roof. In fact, the roof was the lawn.

It had been freshly mown and its cut grass fragrance filled the sunken courtyard. The pond at its centre was alive with croaking frogs. The underground house was totally concealed from the road. No one would have known that it was there without directions. The conversation going on inside was also secret, apparently not for the ears of an inquisitive 12-year-old.

Gingie didn't mind. That was the way with adults after all. As soon as something important cropped up, it had to be kept from you at all costs. It made her wonder why she was there. By the furtive glances at her from the nearby window she assumed it was something she would have been better off not knowing.

Gingie's life had been like that - a complete mystery. Her indulgent, loving parents gave her everything but straightforward answers about her future, making her wonder if she actually had one.

Were they going to give her a sister or brother to play with?

Why should they do that when they had her?

Should she start saving up for her university fees?

She was far too young to start thinking about that. She should be enjoying life while she had the chance.

Why was there so little time to do that?

And so on...

Charlene, her closest friend, had her life plotted out for her before she was five. Gingie just needed to know what the future held for her as well. It sometimes felt as though she had been planted, from another dimension, into the home of Emma and Todd. She was glad about that. They were nice people, much nicer than Charlene's obsessive, possessive parents.

There was something oddly familiar about the courtyard. The enamelled tiles on its walls told tales Gingie felt that she heard before, like other things she knew she should recall, but which just kept slipping away. Todd and Emma always reassured her that it happened to everyone and she should not to worry about it.

The feeling that a long lost friend was waiting for her drew Gingie to the half open door of the room at the far end of the courtyard.

Then she stopped, not quite ready to renew that acquaintance.

But it was too late.

The door opened wide. Inside, the room was filled with lights - the kaleidoscopic lanterns that frequently lit her way into a magical realm. It was so real, Gingie wanted to reach out for the remote control to make it go faster. The walls opened out into a purple heaven. It was always carnival time here. She wanted to dance through the bright lanterns and fly with the scintillating kites scything the sky filled with fireflies. Bizarre creatures in fantastic costumes tweaked her flame coloured hair and spun her around and around until she was giddy.

"Look!" exclaimed Emma. "She's doing it again!"

"Don't worry," Todd said. "She can't come to any harm."

The diminutive old man with glittering eyes said nothing as he watched from the comfort of his patchwork armchair. He could see that Gingie was being swept up in the dancing throng, giggling as she was whirled round and round.

But Emma couldn't. "Oh please, Todd, she's having a fit!"

"No," said the old man. "She's just having fun. You should not disturb her. You know the rules."

"But how long will this go on for?"

"For as long as you insist on keeping her. 12 years and a day - that was the agreement."

"But we can't give her up now," Todd declared firmly.

Gingie continued to twirl about the courtyard, ecstatic in her dream dimension where revellers fluttered about her flaming ginger hair on gossamer wings and showered fairy dust. Gone was the courtyard filled with the fragrance of freshly mown grass and croaking frogs.

It was becoming more and more to tell which world was real. One moment it was life with Emma and Todd, the next this exhilarating whirligig dimension, each time drawing her in deeper.

When the visitors had gone the old man waited until twilight until crossing the courtyard where the sound of mating frogs had grown louder.

"Quiet!" he ordered.

Their amorous croaking immediately stopped.

Cushioned from the noises of the outside world in his sunken home, he entered the room that Gingie had found so enticing. As he crossed its threshold silver cobwebs were illuminated by an eldritch light and, as a bright halo shimmered about his head, the silence was broken by the chatter of tiny voices.

"Well," he said, "are you satisfied with the girl that should have never been?" There was stern disapproval in his tone.

The chattering increased.

"No! It is not possible for you to breathe our life into every stillborn child! This one is confused, no longer sure who she is and can never become an adult. I allowed this just once to prove to you how unwise it was."

The tiny voices became angry.

The old man shrank to his true size and his halo of gold lit up the room.

"Your king has spoken! This will not happen again! Humans and our kind can never mix!"

The chattering died away and the firefly flashes of light skittered back to Nature's realm.

Holidays with Emma and Todd were always

enjoyable. Gingie loved their relaxed company; it made her feel secure. It was not like school where classmates were obsessed with appearance, smartphones and emotional politics. It never occurred to them to enjoy the wonders Nature offered. Had the choice been hers, Gingie would have lived in the woods, listening to birdsong and chattering squirrels, watching the windflowers open and close with the rising and setting of the sun, and piling up dry leaves for badgers to line their sets. She didn't understand why her classmates called her crazy. The natural world seemed a quite sensible place to her.

Charlene was the only one to admire Gingie because she refused to be intimidated by classmates who lived to text, never watch where they were going, and had such tiny outlooks on life. Her existence was fraught in a different way by humourless, controlling parents. It was easy to empathise with the free spirits of Emma, Todd and Gingie. Charlene desperately wanted to accept the invitation to go to the Mediterranean with them on holiday, but her parents forbade it. Instead, she would be confined to that mobile holiday home parked in the dingiest corner they could find of an otherwise glorious countryside for two weeks, especially when it was likely to rain. They both had well-paid jobs and could have afforded to stay at the most expensive hotels with cabarets and saunas. The old saw that those with the most money hang onto it could have been invented for her parents. Oh to have wings and fly away...

The only part of going on holiday Gingie disliked was flying there. She hated being confined in a machine that slashed through the billowing clouds like a polluting spear, making untidy scribbles in the sky with its vapour trail. But then, Gingie hated all vehicles that pumped fumes into the air and overwhelmed Nature's natural fragrances. Emma and Todd were well aware of how she felt and careful to choose a holiday home where everything was within walking distance.

There was something organic about the way the Mediterranean village they selected appeared to have grown from the hillside overlooking an azure blue sea. There were no jet skis or motorboats here. It was safe for fishermen to row out and bring in their nets. Even produce was brought to the local market by donkey and hand carts because the roads were too narrow for cars, and the only way up the hillside was by hundreds of steps.

Gingie felt sorry for the fish: Emma and Todd had given up trying to persuade her to eat animal protein years ago. As soon as they had accepted that, the daughter they never expected to survive bloomed into an extraordinary, beautiful child. Animals, wild and domesticated, recognised a kindred spirit and Emma was sure flowers would turn towards her daughter as she passed. Gingie might not have been an ordinary girl, but every atom of this precious, unworldly creature was theirs... until it had become time for her to leave.

Emma had accepted that she would eventually lose Gingie, but just longed to hold onto her daughter for a little longer. To Todd, it was more of a problem, despite the reassurances of the old man who had magicked her back to life that she would turn into something glorious. Despite everything, he was a realist and could not put his faith in miracles, especially ones beyond his control.

Todd watched Gingie twirling her way across golden Mediterranean sands with Armando, her friend, and other local children happily joining them in the dance. They did not think she was crazy. They somehow knew that this flame-haired girl in the fluttering cotton skirt was special. Even the dolphins would call to her as she skipped along the rickety jetty.

That evening storm clouds rolled in from the sea. Fishermen pulled their boats up the beach and villagers brought in their livestock before going inside to secure the shutters.

Thunder held no terrors for Gingie who giggled excitedly at each lightning strike. Emma persuaded her to leave the porch and watch from the balcony window instead as the heavens released their deluge.

The sky filled with the storm's fiery dragons, illuminating the turbulent sea. Some old houses in the small coastal village were often struck by the lightning.

Emma and Todd took their supper to the back room where the crashing of the storm was not so loud, but Gingie was too exhilarated by

Nature's pyrotechnics to eat anything.

The houses below were on a promontory and taking the full force of the battering wind and rain.

Then the unthinkable happened.

A bolt of lightning struck the roof of Armando's house.

It exploded.

Tiles were scattered by the wind and the ancient rafters burst into flame.

Gingie was horrified. How could Nature be so cruel?

Armando and his family had no cellar to shelter in and dashed from the house as neighbours came out to help them. They all started to point at the balcony overhanging a sheer drop to the crashing waves a hundred metres below. Hanging from its railing was a small figure. Armando must have been fast asleep when the roof was struck and had taken the only way of escape.

But the balcony was starting to come away from the walls. The deluge had doused the fire, but the ancient bricks the railing was bolted to were crumbling.

Emma and Todd dashed out just in time to see Gingie throw open the doors of their balcony. For a second their daughter hesitated.

Then all the strange thoughts that had filled her young life suddenly made sense.

Before Emma and Todd could reach their daughter she raised her arms.

Gingie was engulfed by a brilliant light.

The old man had never told them to expect this.

Huge, opalescent wings unfurled from their daughter's slender back.

With one downbeat she flew up into the storm. Buffeted like a butterfly in the turbulent wind, Gingie reached the petrified Armando just as the railing he was clinging to fell away from the wall.

Gingie caught him before he could fall into the roaring waves below.

His astounded family could not take it what was happening.

As soon as he was flown to their welcoming arms, the apparition that had rescued their son blinked out of sight, leaving a tiny globe of light to dart away into the wind and rain.

Losing Gingie was yet another bereavement for Emma and Todd. But this was different. Although life was going to be empty without the flame-haired child gifted to them by the strange man, the memory of Gingie would remain forever.

A few weeks later they returned to the address on his golden card. The grassy mound was covered with toadstools and mushrooms. Gone was the house with its sunken courtyard and croaking frogs.

The couple were still young enough to adopt a child. There were many they could have given a loving home to, but knew they would never find another Gingie. So they asked Charlene's parents if they could become her godparents, hardly expecting those possessive people to agree.

As they had just lost their child in a tragic accident, and without the chance to bury the body taken by the sea, Charlene's parents agreed. Their daughter would be allowed to spend the occasional weekend with Emma and Todd, which would give them the opportunity to help compensate for the oppressive home life the young teenager had to endure. She was free to play in their small orchard with a neighbour's children, dash under the branches of the apple trees and watch minnows in the stream that ran through the small orchard in the way she had never been allowed to as a child. Charlene relished every moment. Emma and Todd could see why Gingie and her friend had been such kindred spirits.

Charlene's parents became aware that she was changing. She was becoming dreamy and less anxious, so they stopped their daughter visiting her new godparents before she developed the confidence to defy them.

From then on Charlene was watched more closely than ever.

One day the teenager was sitting quietly on the patio that had been prepared for a visit by her father's important business friends. Their daughter's gaze was focused on a small dot of light, which they assumed to be a stray reflection from the cut glass on a nearby table.

Their daughter lifted a finger to touch it.

The light swelled and luminous, opalescent

wings unfurled to envelope Charlene.

There was a tiny 'pop' like a bubble bursting as she disappeared.

Two small globes of light gleefully circled each other for a moment, before darting away into an evening sky filled with fireflies.

Twinkie

This was the first time that Sally had been allowed out on her own, and she had a sneaking suspicion why. Nobody else would take the job.

Given the history of this boarded up old house, it was hardly surprising the other the estate agents didn't want to survey it. Of course, once the property was assessed and had flattering photographs added to a brochure about its amazing potential, older hands would immediately snatch the commission and the credit. Once there was the real chance of a buyer they might even take the customer to view it. With company and a confident sales pitch the place would seem less haunted - not that this part of its history would be mentioned to a potential purchaser.

Sally didn't mind. She was an 18-year-old still learning all the tricks and cunning ways of the house selling business. It was inevitable that she would need to survey a remote, run down property, which had a ghost, at some time or another. Sally just wished it hadn't been this one. Local legend claimed that the sinister rocking horse in the upstairs nursery would sway backwards and forwards accompanied by the wicked giggles of young children. And there it was, looking down from a bay window, glass eyes staring at her as though knowing that it was due to be tossed onto a rubbish dump. Having survived the fire of over one and a half centuries ago, no one had endeavoured to rescue the antique toy. Other furniture and collectible items had long since been salvaged. Once the house had been virtually stripped of fixtures and fittings, that rocking horse remained exactly where it had been on the night of the fire. It was probably that expression... Sally certainly wouldn't have wanted it in her flat, however much of a conversation piece it might have been when entertaining her antique collecting friends. The mythology attached to it alone was enough to give anyone nightmares.

Once the front door was unlocked, enough light escaped through the half boarded-up windows to show the way through the hall. As a precaution against treading on a rotten floorboard, Sally took out her torch.

The dimensions of the downstairs rooms were taken with a laser measure and added to the old plan scanned onto her smartphone. Sally took her time, snapping more photos than necessary, reluctant to ascend the stairs to where the nursery was situated.

A call from her office to check up on how things were progressing meant she could not put off measuring the bedrooms any longer.

Sally ascended the stairs in trepidation. She was surprised to find that the Victorian rooms were light and airy. The fire that had briefly swept through the house had left its charred evidence, but had been quickly doused. Although smoke damaged, the half drawn curtains in the nursery had hardly been scorched and allowed in a shaft of sunlight which fell on... that sinister rocking horse.

Already familiar with its malevolent gaze from the forecourt below, Sally could now feel the toy's evil presence. Part of its mane and tail had been shrivelled by the flames and on the bridle, across its forehead, was the name 'Twinkie'.

To make up the time she had wasted downstairs, Sally quickly measured up the other rooms. The last thing she wanted to do was spend her lunch hour in that house.

Soon, only the nursery remained. Trying not to look at the rocking horse, Sally quickly recorded its dimensions and took a few snaps.

Then Twinkie moved.

Perhaps a freak breeze from the broken window had given him a slight nudge. She was rooted to the spot, but not yet intimidated enough to flee the room.

Then came the high pitched giggling of two young children. It was not the normal, gleeful laughter of infants, but resonated with wickedness.

Rotten floorboards or not, Sally dashed out of the house.

Safely back at her desk, she grabbed a sandwich and mug of tea. Feeling calmer, the trainee estate agent pulled out the folder of documents the current owner of the property had provided. The house had remained unoccupied since the fire one and a half centuries previously. It had been inherited by a distant relative of the owners who lived in Ontario. They only bothered with its basic maintenance and security to prevent it becoming vandalised.

There were foxed pages of copperplate handwriting; too many for anyone else in the office to waste time with. The only thing that interested them was how much the derelict property and its grounds would bring in if sold for redevelopment. Hang the complaints from local historians claiming that it was a local, haunted landmark which should be preserved in all its decaying glory. At one time Sally might have agreed with them, but after her brief experience inside the house it would have been a relief to see it demolished.

At the bottom of the box folder was a large manila envelope containing early police reports. This handwriting was a round, legible print, probably learnt in a 19th-century Mother Hubbard school. At the top of each page was printed the name of a local constabulary and below it the address of the incident. It was surprising that no local historian had managed to ferret out this constable's account of events at that sinister house.

There was no time to read it, so Sally dropped the manila envelope into her briefcase.

There were usually too many distractions after work; Facebook, drinking with friends in the pub, or watching a good film. But that evening something insisted that the contents of the manila envelope were too terrible to be ignored. Sally poured a glass of wine and curled up on the sofa with the police report.

In the autumn of 1865 Constable Flowers had been summoned by the distraught house owner to investigate the sudden and unexplained death of the young nanny he had employed to take care of his four-year-old twin sons. Their mother had died giving birth to them and the father, having to spend so much time away, had gratefully engaged this personable young woman to oversee them. Alice had come from a poor, but respectable, background and was well educated. The rest of the household thought highly of her, even the grumpy housekeeper who could be very territorial.

Dominic and Simon were problem infants, unresponsive to what was going on about them, and had created a small world of their own, which excluded adults and other children alike. Their father had put the identical twins' behaviour down to the fact that they had never known their mother and the small episodes of cruelty exhibited towards family pets and toys merely a phase that would pass.

Immediately he entered the house, Constable Flowers became suspicious of the boys' detached behaviour. Given their tender years it seemed incredible that Dominic and Simon could have been responsible for the death of their new nanny, yet their manner unsettled him. The policeman recommended that the matter should immediately be reported to the coroner. He instructed a medical practitioner to examine Alice's body for traces of noxious substances as there was no other apparent explanation for her death.

The matter was never resolved, and the coroner allowed the young woman to be laid to rest with the other members of her family. A headstone and compensation was donated to the parents by her employer who was reluctant to engage another nanny, although many young women would have been glad of the position. From then on his strict housekeeper kept watch over the twins as she was the only person who could intimidate them into good behaviour.

Relative calm returned to the house for two years.

And then the housekeeper died. There were deep puncture marks in her body. The scullery maid, cook and gardener all lived in fear of this woman and wouldn't have dared confront her with an out of place word, let alone a stiletto blade.

This time Constable Flowers had no doubts and was convinced that Dominic and Simon were responsible. Every moment the policeman spent there, he could feel the needle gaze of four calculating eyes, as the twins' high pitched giggles filled the house. Astride their rocking horse, they swayed to and fro like assassins on the road to their next victim.

Their father had to accept that he had sired two young murderers, and that they should be removed to an institution before they could kill another person.

But Simon and Dominic knew what lay in

store for them. The night before the carriage to take them away was due to arrive, the house caught fire. The local residents and fire brigade quickly quelled the flames before the property was engulfed. The scullery maid, cook and gardener, who lived on the ground floor, were able to escape. But the body of Simon and Dominic's father was found in his bed, hardly touched by the flames.

His throat had been cut while he slept.

The twins had disappeared. Search parties combed the area and daguerreotypes of the six-year-olds were sent to the neighbouring constabularies.

No trace of the children was ever found. The coroner recorded a verdict of death caused by felons unknown, and Constable Flowers must have gone to his grave wondering what became of those little assassins.

Sally finished reading and poured another glass of wine. She didn't sleep very well that night.

The house and land was soon sold for redevelopment. The owners in Ontario did not haggle over the price, well aware of its history and relieved to get rid of it. Despite the protests of local historians, especially when they became aware of the report by Constable Flowers, the developer who had purchased the land demolished the house before the wheels of virtuous preservation could begin to turn.

One overcast morning old rugs, curtains and rotten wood panels were piled up in the forecourt. Twinkie, the malevolent toy of the murderous twins, sat on top of this bonfire, setting its demonic gaze on the demolition team.

Sally watched from the gate as the blaze filled the leaden sky. Constable Flowers would have probably been comforted to know that the rocking horse had been committed to the flames.

Then came an awful, evil, giggling from Twinkie as it was consumed by the inferno. The giggling turned to shrieks that horrified the onlookers.

The rocking horse suddenly exploded in a fireball, releasing two scrolls of black smoke that corkscrewed up into the grey clouds.

www.ingramcontent.com/pod-product-compliance
Lightning Source LLC
Chambersburg PA
CBHW070531130626
46555CB00003B/1365